MW01617220

Carson Clare's Trail Guide to Avoiding Death

And Other Unpleasant Consequences

A Collection of Cautions Designed to Help You Live Life,
Do Stuff, and Possibly Make it Through Middle School

Inspired, Reviled, and Occasionally Disavowed by
Carson McCandless

Painstakingly Composed by
Carson McCandless and
Bruce McCandless III

Fanciful Illustrations Courtesy of
Shaun Venish

ISBN: 0998335118
ISBN 13: 9780998335117

For This Nation's
Oppressed Young People

Special Thanks to Pati, Emma, and Kandice
for Angelic Suggestions
and
Roger G. Worthington,
Minister of Blood and Pulp,
For Everything Else

Dedicated to
Boudica, Joan of Arc,
Aung San Suu Kyi, Malala, Sally Yates,
Wonder Woman, Kathy Switzer,
Rosa Parks, Beatrice MacIlvaine,
Bernice McCandless, Marie Curie,
Ruth Bader Ginsburg, Rachel Carson,
Joan Jett, Berta Caceres, and
All Unfortunate Inmates of
Middle Schools Everywhere

What will you do with your one wild and precious life?

--Mary Oliver

Table of Discontents

Aliens · 1

Anxiety · 3

The Patriarchy · 6

Australia ·10

Cars ·13

Bullies ·14

Revenge ·17

The Cafeteria ·21

Old People · 22

Germs ·24

Grammar ·27

Selfies · 30

Mean Kids ·31

Flamingos · 36

Social Media ·38

School · 40

Nazis ·41

Indecision · 43

Robots ·45

Geography ·47

Sharks ·50

Siblings ·52
Body Shamers ·53
Boogers · 60
Steamed Vegetables ·62
Zombies ·65
Some Additional Horrors ·67

Aliens

We know they're lurking around out in space.
It's a matter of math. The probabilities shout it.
What we can't understand about our alien friends
Is why they're determined to make us all doubt it.

With a million planets out there good for living,
Why are our neighbors so shy about giving
Us just a quick glimpse of their tentacled faces,
Or the flickering gleam of their sleek carapaces?

Or their luminous distended fibrous lungs?
Or the sentient creatures who live on their tongues?
Are their claws made of carbon, or crazier stuff?
When will they figure we've been patient enough?

ON THE OTHER HAND:

What if, when they go to give us a hug,
They transmit some creepy carnivorous slug
That worms into our ears, all toothy and wet,
Slimy, translucent, like a nightmare's pet,
To ingest our cerebrums and suck in our eyes
And munch on our membranes like gray matter pies
Till we shriek with horror and pointless regret?
On second thought, maybe we'll wait a while yet.

Danger Rating: Speculative, but possibly cataclysmic. And really gross (*see eye-sucking, above*)

Survival Tips:

- Avoid contact with hideous aliens (unless they're family)
- Encourage development of new Pentagon laser technologies
- Hide under the bed—they never look there

Anxiety

The snooze bone rests
just in front of the back,
near the buoyancy bulb
and the sympathy sack—

either of which
can generate trouble
if punctured or prodded,
squashed or bent double.

But worse is the loss
of this zigzagorous bone
that comforts the cranky
and welcomes her home.

With no viable bone
to soothe one to sleep,
one's worries start stacking
themselves in a heap

till finally the pile
is as big as a redwood.
You get to school angry
and don't go to bed good.

Your visions hightail it
for other soft heads,
to "dance their endancements,"
as someone once said.

At least the snooze bone
is easily tended.
Don't try to sleep nervous,
or till your mad's ended.

Just let this odd item
expand in your chest.
(It works in a lawn chair,
but supine is best.)

Don't summon deep thoughts.
Be quiet. They'll come.
Your brain will unbungle,
your bone start to hum

till your room fades to black
and bright stars crowd around,
and the voices beneath you
aren't making a sound.

WELCOME, DREAM SAILOR!
Now steer for the sea,
where all that you hope for
meets all you will be.

Danger Rating: Low-grade, but persistent

Survival Tips:

- Sleep when you can—that's where the dreams are
- Sip chamomile tea to enhance drowsiness
- Attend local school board meetings

The Patriarchy

If you were born female
(and if so, *HUZZAH!*)

here's something you'll see
that may stick in your craw:

the inclination of men
to make women believe

that they're lesser somehow.
It happened to Eve,

who was blamed by her mate
for a diet decision

that led to the couple's
sweet lease deal rescission.

But who wrote that tale?
Can you answer, "MEN"?

And who was around
to take statements back then?

The fact of the matter is,

men have long tried,
by hook and by crook,

to keep women down
on the basis of looks

and whether we coddle
the egos of dudes

and admire their muscles.
These lame attitudes

worked for zillions of years!
Women were chattel—

couldn't *own*, couldn't *vote*—
we were bartered like cattle

and made to work for low pay.
It's still done that way

in lots of earth's regions,
and some think it's okay

but others of us
are determined to state

that women are equals,
and equals don't wait

for others to *give*
what is rightfully ours—

not one more mad minute,
not one more long hour.

We can do just what
our brothers can do,

and sometimes do it better
(it hurts, but it's true).

So girls, mind the menace
that's held us so long,

the gray-bearded peril
that's reaped so much wrong:

the habit of men to
put us in fetters.

It worked for a while,
but now we know better.

These bonds aren't of iron.
They're made in the mind.

Only now they are breaking.
Because NOW is our time.

Danger Rating: Relentless, though occasionally difficult to detect

Survival Tips:

- Believe you can do it—because you can

Australia

The Ozzies are a good-natured race,
which helps to disguise what a horrible place
is the land they inhabit. It's really a wonder
those folks can even stay *upright* down under.

It's a land mass designed by a succubus—
an ark made by imps—the back of God's bus—
the dark side of town—Earth's animal ghetto,
where monsters warm up for a grisly libretto.

This is no place for *hakuna matata*;
It's home to *hapalochlaena lunulata*
And *lasseldectus hasseltii*,
And other ten-dollar words for "goodbye."

There's the dreaded box jelly, the pickleback spider,
the saltwater croc, and the giant black tiger.
All manner of things that are bad here get badder.
(That slithering shadow? THAT'S A DEATH ADDER.)

Even the stonefish, for the love of Pete.
a creature that closely resembles concrete,
and moves at roughly the speed of ground,
can easily strike a grown man down.

Since ¾ of the fauna you see will assail ya,
and not even the stoutest first-aid will avail ya,
unless you're decked out in tungsten regalia,
it's probably best to steer clear of Australia!

Danger Rating: 63% of tourists visiting Australia die within four hours of arrival.

Survival Tips:

- Try New Zealand

Note: 74% of statistics completely fabricated by authors.

Cars

Run over, crushed, or pinned inside,
locked in as the temperature starts to rise,

compelled by an inopportune collision
to speak with an oncoming Buick's transmission:

more kids are killed each year in cars
than soldiers die in foreign wars.

You can talk about tanks or missile barrages.
The real threat lurks nearby, in garages—

two streamlined tons of oil and steel,
not shot from a barrel but steered by a wheel.

And soon you'll get your license to drive it!
Let's all say a prayer. Perhaps you'll survive it.

Danger Rating: Extremely High

Survival Tips:

- Don't ride in vehicles with idiots
- Take bus when available
- If your gut says walk, *run*

Bullies

The style of bullies varies by gender.
(*It's been said before, I'll confess.*)
You're more likely to get a fist to the head
from a dude than someone in a dress.

Boy bruisers are hairy, quick-tempered, and vile.
Their voices are frequently set at eleven.
Their names are Big Frank, Hakeem, and Alberto;
You're usually safe with a Milo or Kevin.

But girls have their own, less obvious ways
To enforce what they see as the laws;
Note the whispered aside, the tittering laugh,
And the "helpful" appraisal of flaws.

It's all designed to keep the world stable—
To prevent kids from rising or changing.
The bully wants to remain where she is,
And is scared of the world rearranging.

There's no surefire way to avoid the attacks
Of queen bees and Blutos—both pinheaded jerks.
Sometimes you adapt; sometimes you fight back;
Sometimes you *run*, if nothing else works.

And sometimes you simply put your head down
And wait for stupidity's storm to re-route.
Bullies have short shabby violent careers.
In high school, they start to figure this out.

See, there's no real revenge. It doesn't exist.
But there's a victory better by far:
Never surrender the *something* inside you.
Do what you have to. Become who you are.

Danger Rating: Significant, and Extremely Tiresome

Survival Tips:

- Boys: Avoid weight room when football or wrestling team in proximity
- Also swim team
- Girls: Find real friends; don't sweat what the other ones say

Revenge

There once was a girl who's no longer a girl
(in fact, Cassie's making her way in the world)
who went to the zoo. But not any old zoo!
This was a zoo for strange creatures who

promised all manner of magical pay-back
for bad things she'd suffered far-off in her way-back,
from bullies who said she would always be fat,
to fake friends who laughed that she wasn't all that.

There in stout cages for all to observe
were numerous nightmares who were eager to serve:
trolls and hobgoblins, gray spectres and creeps,
shadow men making fantastical leaps.

Foremost was a werewolf, husky and hirsute,
a ferociously nasty, salivating galoot
who begged for release so he could help Cassie out
by taking revenge on one particular lout

who'd offended our girl in various ways
on the day she tried out for the junior high play.
Why, he'd tear him *apart*! He'd snack on his *spleen*!
He'd make him pay plenty, if you know what I mean.

And it really was tempting. The wounds still hurt.
There were people she wanted to grind into dirt.
A cheerleader, for instance. Her History teacher.
A basketball coach, the hideous creature.

And these were precisely the beasts that could do it.
All she needed to do was give in and pursue it.
Here was a gremlin. Over there you could find
a couple of mummies where they tried to unwind;

and Frankenstein's bride, a woman of parts;
a Dr. Hank Jekyll, of particular smarts;
and vampires, redcaps, and various ghosts,
who promised to bring her what she wanted most.

When they saw little Cassie was starting to waver,
the beasts got excited. They started to slaver.
They screamed at the bars that kept them in cages
in highly theatrical murderous rages.

But in the midst of this highly unharmonious din,
Cassie remembered a very shy friend
who once held her hand when she started to cry
over something or other; she didn't know why.

And this echo of caring on a cancerous day
made her think of a boy who'd gone out his way
to say a sweet something about her old shoes
at a time she was drowning in ocean-sized blues.

The thought of these deeds was a voice from afar
that spoke as the werewolf battered his bars.
It said, *recollect those who have done you some kindness*
before you succumb to this species of blindness.

But that isn't all young Cassie was hearing.
The ghouls and the nixies were hissing and jeering:
Why are you waiting? We know what you're here for!
Take charge of your life, and open this door!

Without saying a word, she declined to unlock it.
She put the black key back into her pocket,
and headed due west for the wrought-iron gate
(the one marked FORGIVENESS; not the one that said HATE).

And she never went back to that nightmare zoo,
though sometimes she found herself wanting to,
because, all manner of self-serving claptrap aside,
the zoo's where such beasties should always abide.

Monsters, you see, have a really bad trait.
Once they're let out, they remain in that state.
Once they're set free, they don't care who they maim;
monsters are legendarily hard to re-tame.

So Cassie will tell you, if you have vengeance designed,
to keep these vile creatures locked up in your mind.
Revenge is quite tempting to wonder about,
and the monsters are calling. But don't let them out!

Danger Rating: Subtle, but corrosive

Survival Tips:

- Not forgiving is like drinking rat poison and then waiting for the rat to die. (Anne Lamott)

The Cafeteria

If you've been lucky, or totally blessed,
Perhaps you've avoided the hideous mess
We've been getting for lunch these days at our school.
It's not always awful, but it is as a rule.

It's like, goat guts and gravy sealed in a can,
Beans—mostly navy—from Afghanistan,
And tamales constructed of something unknown
(Though whatever it was, it had tiny bones).

You can bring lunch from home, if your mother will make it,
And the dog doesn't eat it, or you forget to take it,
But what if you don't? And what if you're starvin'
And get stuck in the line behind Bug-Eatin' Marvin

And notice the ladies who preside at the oven
Have convened like a cackling soup kitchen coven
To laugh at the thought of what they're serving today
Just as your "rice pilaf" starts crawling away.

Who the heck is Salisbury? And why is he steak?
Who said zucchini could be made into cake?
Is this fruit with bruises? Or bruises with fruit?
And why does the chili smell like your foot?

Surely the taxes good citizens pay
Can fund salad that's green, not gummy and gray?
Few of us like to seem surly or rude,
But come on, people! Can we get some real food?

Old People

Their breath smells like trash cans.
They grunt when they walk.
You can see what they've eaten
For lunch when they talk.

They're nervous on car rides,
And clamp onto your hands.
They don't know the difference
Between good and bad bands.

They squint when they read.
They can't text at all.
You're always half-scared and
Half-hoping they'll fall.

But the real problem's not just
That they're warty and slow;
That they hog both the bathrooms
And have to constantly *go*.

Far worse than their hacking
Up truck loads of phlegm?
One day you'll wake up and
Find out that you're *them*.

Danger Rating: WHAT?

Survival Tips:

- Still working on this one

Germs

You wouldn't be here if it
weren't for this fact: You're a
long-term hotel for
microbial flora.

They're unseemly things,
but guess what? Germs are *good*.
It would be dumb to evict them
(and it's not clear you could).

Nine hundred species
call our intestines their home.
Another large horde
surfs our mucosal foam.

They need us, no doubt.
We're like their own earth.
They've been traveling with us
from the day of our birth.

Sure, there are some
to avoid when you can,
like unicellular forms
of the grim Taliban—

Vibrio vulnificus, the
flesh-eating bacteria;
malaria; cholera;
Streptococcus; listeria—

but most go to work
every day like your elders;
good decent farmers
and trash men and welders.

They break down food protein
and help to digest it,
sense the growth of bad bugs
and help to arrest it,

provide vitamins for us,
and essential enzymes.
In short, germs aren't pests,
they're our partners in grime.

So let's drink from cupped hands
and not from a glass.
Let's wade into mud and
roll around in green grass.

Let's get ourselves funky
and if someone asks why,
say we do it for dirt,
and *escherichia coli*!

Danger Rating: Unavoidable

Survival Tips:

- Relax. A little schmutz is good for you, immunologically speaking
- Get a dog—they're totally filthy

Grammar

the case of the child
who always appended
a hopeful conjunction
where each statement ended

did not make the papers
much less the late news
few folks seemed to care much
about her odd views

and yet there were those
(like myself, I confess)
who waited in alleys
to hear her profess

her philosophy of
the Indivisible Now:
I've given up periods
will no longer allow

their detestable dot
that rotund little dam
to keep all that could be
from things as they stand

see whatever has happened
will happen again
the cries they hear there
are cries you'll hear then

so I'd much rather stitch a
grammatical suture
some link from what has been
straight into the future

and that is why I
prefer in these things
to always add AND
to all of my endings and

They shut down her meetings.
The State gave her a sentence.
These harsh words were posted
at every town entrance:

THE VIOLENCE ON TV
HAS NOTHING TO DO
WITH THE VIOLENCE SOON
TO BE VISITING YOU.

WHAT HAPPENS IN ONE PLACE
IS NOT HAPPENING HERE.
THAT'S THE END OF THE STORY.
THERE'S NOTHING TO FEAR.

they deleted her colon
they undotted her i's
she slipped into a comma
and was then euphemized

still we remember
the girl who broke cages
who wouldn't leave sentences
nailed to white pages

who introduced then
to what's happening now
tied all starts to this finish
welded stern to the bow

the world keeps on spinning
each wave shapes the beach
the river won't behave
and neither should speech

like a wall made of pin pricks
like a castle of sand
their dots won't divide us
we swear it

The And

Danger Rating: Mostly metaphorical

Survival Tips:

- Grammar is a kind of prison; don't let 'em correct you to death

Selfies

We've got cellular towers throughout the land
so please take more selfies whenever you can.

It's crucial to capture the moods you go through.
You might look different in a moment or two,

So posture and pose wherever you go—
London, Chicago, or New Mexico.

If you ever stop in to see the Grand Canyon,
step over that rail and find something to stand on.

So what if you stumble while holding your phone?
At least we'll have selfies of you when you're gone.

Just pooch out those lips—show people you got 'em!
And try to keep pouting all the way to the bottom.

Danger Rating: Manageable

Survival Tips:

- Take pics from above, never below, for most flattering looks
- Tie self to car when taking selfies in mountainous regions

Mean Kids

It was common knowledge in our part of town
(and in other precincts it was going around)
that no kid liked playing with Hillary Snow
because of the way that she carried on so
whenever she felt as if she'd been slighted.
It didn't take much to get her excited.

A toy in the arms of another young friend
was enough to send Hillary off 'round the bend,
fussing and fighting, kicking and biting.
For miles around there'd be buses colliding,
for the sound of her screams was famously known
to carry a highly unsettling tone

that made people want to yank out their hair—
to slobber like monkeys—to gibber and stare
till whatever young Hillary wanted at last
was given back into her tight little grasp.
To most other children it didn't seem righteous
that Hillary prospered while so impoliteous.

In fact, Sid Gollub and Diego McDivitt
and Farley O'Slubb and Myrtle Rae Trivett
begged their parents not to make them appear
at Hillary's house for her birthday each year.
But this time was different. The word got around
that Hillary's folks had sat the tyke down

and pleaded with Hillary please to be nice.
Because they knew pleading might not suffice,
they also tried bribing their nettlesome daughter
with gewgaws and gifties they'd secretly bought her
and others they promised, of every description:
a desperate last measure; a slim-chance prescription.

But the promises *did* seem to make an impression.
The girl and her parents emerged from that session
with a solid accord: no screaming, no shrieking,
no flops to the floor while others were speaking.
She'd act like a lady—her word was her bond—
and be well-rewarded. At last the day dawned.

Oh, how the sun sparkled! And how the kids cheered!
For the party was nothing at all like they'd feared.
They could play with whatever toys they enjoyed—
With Fantastical Space Bombs! With Slippery Floyd!
With a Pneumatic Goo Maker (CAUTION: REAL GOO)
and a diaphanous electronic didgeridoo!

It's hard to say now just what happened that day,
but the cause was a simple one, some people say.
Hillary realized that the children who'd come—
not some, but all eighty—were having more fun
than she was—and she was, you see, the *point* of it all,
the center of everything, belle of the ball,

and to see, just to *witness*, Myrtle Rae Trivett
laughing and dancing made Hillary livid.
Why was O'Slubb turning flips in the air
off the pool's diving board while everyone stared?
This was her party! Her once-yearly bash!
So forget the danged pony! All the grimy green cash!

Her parents were more than usually frightened
to see how Hill's anger rapidly heightened.
She drew back her shoulders, her arms and her knees.
She tensed up her innards. She squelched a large sneeze.
She swelled like a tire that's been blown up too tight,
or a water balloon bulging on Halloween night.

It's difficult here not to be somewhat graphic.
As authorities quickly rerouted air traffic,
Hill twirled like a sprinkler dousing the grass.
She jerked like a demon attending high mass.
And this was a doozie, a real humfaloodler;
Nothing folks shouted even seemed to get through to her.

And so little Hill unleashed her last tantrum,
a seizure unmatched by any panjandrum
or chubby-cheeked princeling or monarch of old.
The sight was enough to turn torrid blood cold.
As she started to glow like a ripe *habanero,*
Sid Gollub screamed, "Git! She's fixin' to BLOW!"

and sure enough, upward did Hillary geyser,
fragments of torso like stars in the sky, sir.
And as gravity started pulling them low
all the happy kids shouted, "It's HILLARY snow!"
From that time till this, it's been part of her fame:
no two flakes of that girl looked exactly the same.

The aim of this poem is not to cause tension,
nor even to rattle with metrical mention
all those in our ranks who have not learned to share.
It's simply to show, for all who may care,
how a mean little child—*Tyrannis, sic semper!*—
exploded herself with a very bad temper.

Danger Rating: Mild (but persistent, with increasing risk of headache)

Survival tips:

- Avoid selfish jerks. They might blow up. Or take your stuff
- Give till it hurts—but no more

Flamingos

While it's never wise to risk an attack
by our friend the noble flamingo,
it's better to flirt with this sort of pain
than the bite of the jaguar or dingo

or the sting of the Peruvian predator wasp
(which they say can leave a hideous rash)
or the wrath of the Burmese black-bottomed ape
(be prepared for a possibly gangrenous gash).

However, you still want to mind
your manners with 'mingos, my friends,
for to trifle with even God's mildest creatures
is generally liable to lead to bad ends.

Here, it's not just the pain that could come
from a brutal, but justified, beaking.
It's also the lifetime larded with shame,
for not to be coarse in how I am speaking,

it would be ever so hard to explain—
for a manly man, I should certainly think—
being chased through a swamp and then injured
by something so skinny (not to mention so *pink*)!

Danger Rating: Whimsical

Survival Tips:

- Maybe be cool to flamingos?
- Also whooping cranes

Social Media

The future you's watching the present-day you
And hoping to send you a message, or two,
That will probably never make its way through,
But here's what the authors are willing to do:

We'll pass it on for yous (no need for odd looks;
It's a service that comes when you purchase the book).[1]
It turns out the future-you's really quite cool
With the way you've handled yourself while in school.

Despite what you see on InstaFaceTubeChat,
On Lickit and ScopeMe and HeyLookaThat,
There's no cause to go making yourself all morose
Comparing yourself to smartphones full of ghosts.

You're just the right height! You're not scary skinny.
Your acne's short-term; your laugh's not a whinny.
Your legs work quite well. Your eyebrows are fine.
There's nothing so strange in the curve of your spine.

You're not too slothful—you've just enough *sloth*—
You don't breathe like a beast from the ice planet, Hoth
(Well, sometimes you do, but only when running),
And your good morning smile is really quite stunning.

---

[1] Offer not valid in Nebraska.

The future you's sitting on a boat in the bay,
And watching the tide wash the evening away,
Or standing alone as the sky droops with stars,
And she barely remembers old middle school scars.

She sends you this missive: Don't worry. No fear.
I'll be waiting to hold you as soon as you're here.
What she thinks, with a sigh, looking back from afar,
Is you're perfect—I'm *awesome*—just as we are.

Danger Rating: Mostly mild, with occasional eruptions of envy and self-doubt

Survival Tips:

- Unplug already
- Remember: everyone's entitled to the moon and the stars

School

Young sparrows spill from streetlight poles
    to conquer avenue trees,
and monarchs drift above the fields,
    blown northward on the breeze.
The dandelions have lost their heads.
    The dogs trade secret smiles.
The clover's holding special sales
    and bees jam all the aisles.
September seemed too tired to talk.
    December droned all day.
February warned us not to laugh.
    At last, my friends, we May.

Danger Rating: Numbs mind, steals soul. Could be worse

Survival Tips:

- Occasionally pretend you have no idea what anyone's talking about; this will prepare you for life after graduation

Nazis

The littlest Nazi, Alice Green,
grew up with dreams inside her head
that girls like her were better girls
and other girls were better dead.

Not that she practiced violence—
most nights, she practiced violin.
But she was not afraid to praise
the virtues of her snow-white skin.

It simply seemed to Alice Green
that fair complexions and blue eyes
implied a better sort of mind.
All else was dingy pious lies.

And so small people grew enraged
and several chased her through the town,
while others filed civil suits
and tried to wear her family down

till one day Alice turned around
and quieted the ringing taunts.
*All children ought to have the right
to say and think the way they want,*

quoth Alice Green. *This is my creed.
We learn it every year in school
and you may hate me for my thoughts
but I will not live by mob rule.*

And so she stood and dared the crowd
to strike a slender eight year-old
who'd simply tried to live her life
as best she heard what conscience told.

And no one there, of any hue,
could stand to smash that pretty face—
behind which worked a heart and mind
of just the same stuff as their race.

The wisest there said, *Leave her be.*
She simply speaks as she believes.
We cannot make her love us all
or take her thoughts like palace thieves.

So Alice Green was given hugs,
and all assembled made a vow
to let each other live in peace.
And so I will, she thought. *For now.*

Danger Rating: Trending higher.

Survival Tip:

- Avoid organizations that treat people differently based on what they
  look like or try (peacefully) to believe
- Don't trust fascists—white, brown, or black

Indecision

A dozen men set sail one day
aboard the *Irresolute*.
The men were found outside Bombay
years later, picking jute.

What befell you? each was asked.
What went so horribly wrong?
The captain changed his mind, said one,
and headed for Hong Kong.

Wasn't *that*, another chimed,
that cost us name and pay.
It was the way the second mate
so longed to see Marseilles.

The mate he answered Captain, no,
you've got to stop that talk.
The crew caused our maladies
by making for Bangkok!

The scholars softly stole away,
not caring to stay till the end.
All argument ceased at 9:45,
and then promptly started again.

Danger Rating: Debatable

Survival Tips:

- Make a decision already!

Robots

We made the machines to increase our reach:
To roam underseas and crunch long calculations;
To spot-weld our Chevys and analyze tumors;
To get us to Mars so we could start exploration.

But the better they got, the more we deferred.
Soon there was nothing they couldn't do faster.
They lasered our eyeballs, and fashioned our high balls,
And took over planning for major disasters.

They weren't quite as good at writing our songs,
But the Springsteen 3000 was coming along,
And eventually all that we needed to do
Could be easily scheduled from noon until two.

And then all the things that we *wanted* to do
Were made strictly off limits. It was for our own good.
We weren't quite as smart or as safe as we could be.
We hadn't been living the way *they* thought we should.

Finally we were asked just to stand to one side.
Wisdom came slowly, and a little too late.
And though our learning accrued over years,
The lesson was really quite easy to state:

The greater the number of things done *for* you,
The less you can manage to do for yourself.
The fewer the things you're able to do,
The more you will need their mechanized help.

You see the dilemma? Can you tell where it leads?
Are warm-blooded companions among robotic needs?
Let's hope there's a place in the folds of tomorrow
For things that we humans are good at: like sorrow.

Danger Rating: We're doomed

Survival Tips:

- Stay off the grid
- KILL ALL ROBOTS!
- If tip above doesn't work: OBEY ALL ROBOTS!

Geography

Why can't the naming
of the world make sense?
In Texas there are *Texans*.
It's easy to declense.
With Iowa it's similar:
the pural adds an "ans."
But many countries nowadays
are filled with arrogance:
with their *eni*s and their *ecia*s
and their phonic indiscrecia,
it's enough to make a student
wanna knock a little sense in
every Grecian or Slovecian
or bypassing Indonecian
who is certain to be bothered
by the slightest of offense!

When the globe was somewhat newer,
seems like nations were far fewer.
You could disregard Croatians,
had no Serbs to try your patience,
and the Uzbeks were a twinkle in
some jolly mullah's eye. Why
Burma's now Myanmar!
Which would make my old gryanmar
buy a ticket for Ceylon,
'cept Ceylon is now long gone—

it's been ousted by Sri Lanka,
which has caused no little ranka
among the folks who thought they knew
what the heck was going on!

The *stans* are largely trans-
Caucasian, carved from heat and dust.
Afghans think it's quite okay there—
maybe any desert dweller must.
Many *iria*s are found around
the African exteria:
Algeria, Nigeria, Liberia, and such.
There's nonetheless Siberia,
Which doesn't fit at all (or much).
The *anians* are everywhere:
It's hard to find a rule.
Rumanians, Iranians,
Albanians, Bahranians:
it's enough to make a student
claw her eyes and start to drool.

If the boys and girls of Poland
are the folks we know as *Polish*,
then it follows that in Holland
the residents are—*Holish*?
That's the sort of gaffe, we're told,
that really leaves the UN cold.
But surely it can be acknowlished
geographic logic's minimalish.

Guinea's sitting up hear Ghana.
Neither one is near Guyana,
which is further still removed from Georgia
(not the Georgia with Atlanta,
but the Georgia with Tblisi).
Why can't we take it easy?

I don't care to make things dumber,
and school shouldn't be for slumber,
but I'd long much less for summer
if every nation had a NUMBER.

Danger Rating: Generally mild, though occasionally more serious at international airports

Survival Tips:

- Avoid locales associated with the term "truck bomb"—like countries 33, 41, and 109
- And sometimes 68
- North Dakota is nice this time of year

Sharks

With his sandpaper skin and bloodthirsty snoot,
he'll join you in your bathing suit

but not to swim. He's done all that.
He's a big fan of your body fat.

For him there's no difference between panic and play.
He can hear your heart beating a mile away.

His teeth are sharp, and slice through bone
to leave two holes where your legs had grown,

so of evolution's many boons,
give loud hosannas for this one—

while sharks may claim to rule the waves,
thank God they never learned to *run*.[2]

Danger Rating: Worth considering

Survival Tips:

- Stay away from Australia (see "Australia," above)

---

[2] Another cool thing to ponder on: We seem to have missed the Megalodon.

Siblings

I've heard big sisters can be the best,
But mine is mostly a giant pest.
Kicking, taunting, shrieking, screaming:
For all of this effort, there is no meaning.
BOY PROBLEMS! HORMONES!
THE CRISIS DU JOUR!
Sisters are what locks
Were invented for.
Where once you'd beg her
To come and play,
Now you wish she'd *go away*.

Siblings are basically, I think, no fun.
I suspect that's true for everyone.

Danger Rating: Minimal (unless being annoying is carcinogenic)

Survival Tips:

- Sell objectionable sibling to circus (or trade for baboon)

Body Shamers

Of all the light sleepers and midnight creepers
who anxiously wait for the yuletide,
there was one named Miranda
who swore she'd catch Santa
and one year her moment arrived.

She lived near Atlanta, our ambitious Miranda,
where she owned a cool gym called HARD CORE.
She drank seven Red Bulls.
She did some light lat pulls
and shivasana-ed out on the floor.

Close on to dawn, the Big Man plopped down
in a flurry of cinders and embers.
He was chilled from his ride.
It was freezing outside!
(Recall, this took place in December.)

When he'd done the gift set-out, he turned for his get-out,
but Miranda was ready and poised.
She leapt up from the rug
to give Santa a hug,
and said, "Kringle, step away from the toys!

"I've got something to ask you—I'm taking to task you
for not letting us know where you're at.
Can't we just for once *see* you?
Won't you give us a wee view?"
Sighed Santa, "I would, but I'm FAT.

"I can barely get airborne; I snore like an air horn;
my knees are beginning to give.
My wife's crullers with nuts
have inflated my butt.
Is this how a legend should live?

"I'm getting mean texts, each more cruel than the next,
that opine that my weight's out of hand.
I don't walk, I waddle—
I'm an awful role model—
I'm a joke and I ought to be banned."

Miranda then struck; she said, "You're in luck!"
I'm a certified personal trainer.
I can make you quite fit
(you'll be sore where you sit).
All I need is a monthly retainer."

And so it began, Miranda's big plan
to make Santa Claus shapely and svelte.
She got him weight-lifting—
said it would help with his gifting,
and save him a bundle on belts.

St. Nick hit the gym, and the gym it hit him
like a truck load of steel kettle bells.
Santa worked out his abs
till his gut was a slab
and he slowly slipped out of his shell.

He rarely ate dinner as he kept growing thinner
but the protein shakes were delicious.
He kept getting stronger!
His long runs got longer!
And the smell of baked goods seemed seditious.

There was one problem, though, and it started to grow
as Kris Kringle got muscled and godlike.
He was no longer around
in Santa Claus town
and all agreed it was odd, like,

that when he finally did show, it was only to go
rummaging through all the gift lists.
He scratched out the toys
for the good girls and boys
and opined that the whole lot was shiftless:

"It's not up for debate; not *one's* lifting weights,
and I won't toss my gifts to teen slackers.
I want each of these kids
to do just as I did.
I'll enlist all their parents as backers."

"Little Sara wants dollies; well, she's out of luck.
She's just getting wheat germ, poor dear.
I've been spinning like crazy
while she's being lazy.
I'll be giving out FitBits this year."

So Santa grew cross, and obsessed with weight loss,
and counting his caloric intake.
He told the elves to be quiet,
put Mrs. Claus on a diet—
it was more than the North Pole could take!

Sure he was quicker; no one would bicker
with the results Miranda had gotten.
But what was the point
if everyone in the joint
was suddenly feeling so rotten?

Santa was heedless; he said, "We'll all *feed* less
and then everything will be fine."
But one little elfess
was particularly selfless
and had been wanting to talk this whole time.

She was a tiny young girl with a tiny young curl,
but her voice rang out chime-like and true.
She said, "Boss, you're much fitter,
But you've also grown bitter.
What you've lost was the best part of you."

There was silence that day, and the skies they were gray
as Santa stood sullen and sleek.
But this lass, like Miranda,
she loved her some Santa,
and a bright tear escaped down her cheek.

She barely had teeth! She was frightened of beef!
You could blow her away with a sneeze.
But this spunky elf, Maya,
had rekindled a fire
and Santa Claus dropped to his knees.

A man's heart is his heart, right from the start,
and the heart as we know is a muscle.
And Santa realized
as he watched the girl cry
that he'd missed something huge as he hustled.

In all of his sweating, he'd started forgetting
that Christmas is not about numbers.
Christmas is giving
all the sweetest kids living
a blessing at night while they slumber.

Quoth Kringle: "Gadzooks! Who cares how I look?"
We are creatures of soul, not of silk!
There's no time to yammer!
Let's grab our toy hammers!
Someone set out the cookies and milk!

"Out to the workshop! It's time to go non-stop,
to make sure we've got enough loot
to shower on kiddies
in all the world's cities.
Now where is that giant red suit?"

Santa never backslid to the things he once did,
like eating four hams at a go.
But he did moderate
(i.e., *he regained some weight*—
it's warmer that way in the snow).

Now I'm happy to say the Big Man's on his way.
He's recovered from Miranda's regime.
He's back in fine form,
his cheeks jolly and warm,
and he'll visit this year while you dream.

And as for Miranda? She's back in Atlanta,
and leaner than ever, they say.
She'll train you, of course.
You'll be as strong as a horse!
But will you be *nicer* that way?

Danger Rating: Increases with age

Survival Tips:

- If exercise seems imminent, stuff pockets with emergency bacon
- Support gluten-based tax incentives

Boogers

It's nature's own Play-Do,
a bacterial ball
that's smeared under desks,
on lockers, in stalls

like organic graffiti,
like membranous murals
mashed to make gumdrops
or daubed in thick swirls.

Most girls can't stand
the sight of a booger,
but some dudes will harvest
and eat them like sugar,

so beware of the *hombre*
who dotes on his nose.
That's where it's cooking.
That's whar she blows!

The gym floor geode.
The comb-toter's crack.
Seventh grade sea salt.
The mouth breather's snack.

So warm and elastic,
I'm not being snarktastic,
I've seen it produced,
this mucosal juice

perfect for forming
smooth flying spheres
that have been the clear cause of
much shrieking and tears.

It's not just a taboo!
There's science here too.
You can get *hepatitis*
from the fruit of the sinus,

but gross will be gross,
just as boys will be boys,
and some will continue
to make their own toys.

Danger Rating: Not so severe, unless you really hate to vomit

Survival Tips:

- Wear raincoat at all times
- Leave loose change under couch and car seats
- Proceed immediately to high school

Steamed Vegetables

Few nematodes have passed my lips.
At least, few that I saw.
I've yet to sample sun-dried boots
or taste stir-fried macaw.

Still I would opt for each of these
and ingest them all with glee
before I'd take another bite
of boiled broccoli.

The Tree of Death, the Zulus say,
declining to speak more.
Peru has passed a stringent law
to keep it out of stores.

And only in America
are folks coerced to try it.
The FDA's dead set upon
the shrub's place in our diet.

Bratwurst chompers! Patriots!
Know what your government's about.
The tree of death's a stalking horse—
a front for Brussels sprouts!

And German beans, and Swiss-grown kale,
and Asia's beastly chard.
Soon there won't be any place
for beef, potatoes, lard,

or chocolate cake, or Little Debs,
or moose heads in the den.
These greens will be the death of us.
Abolish the U.N.!

Danger Rating: Unclear (authors have never eaten vegetables)

Survival Tip:

- Stick Brussels sprouts in pants till coast is clear

Zombies

It's Hollywood's fault. I don't mean to spite 'em,
but they've done zombies, now, *ad finitum*:

zombies that sprint; zombies that shamble;
Zombies in Love (now *that* was a gamble),

Old-timey creepers, deadbots from space,
Zombies consuming the whole human race.

But it's really quite simple. Remember these words
if the mundane should one day become the absurd:

The biggest problem with zombies remains
their predilection for eating brains.

If *you've* got extra smarts to spare,
by all means go ahead and share,

but for those of you attached to your heads,
avoid provoking the living dead.

Get inside and lock the doors!
Board up all windows on ground-level floors!

Like everyone else, the dead have to eat—
and the world has a finite supply of meat.

Danger Rating: Largely Hypothetical (but what do the "scientists" know?)

Survival Tips:

- Don't experiment on human beings or other anthropoids with unknown, rabies-like viruses
- Stay out of graveyards—especially if you see grimy hands like, *clawing out of the earth*
- Get fit; foot speed is gonna count with these critters

Some Additional Horrors

Periodically space rocks fall from the sky,
As three did in Kansas one Fourth of July.
There's not a whole lot a person can do.
Be glad that crater wasn't formerly *you*.

Bad things attend us from the day of our birth,
But there's a reason we're currently crowding the earth.
Catastrophes happen; but mostly they don't.
We could die any day, but most of us won't.

Some unlikely dangers: a rampaging squid;
Meteor showers; the katydid;
Invaders from space, and monsters from Mars;
Kid-eating catfish; alligator gars;

Velociraptors revived in a lab;
Some strange walking dead thing, conceived on a slab;
Slime from the ice machine; demonic cars;
A revivified T-rex; bugs from the stars;

Volcanic eruption; age-addled czars;
The bubonic plague; that dude with the scars;
Massively radioactive lizards;
Ferociously clever boarding school wizards.

You could die from a dramatically age-weakened bungee.
Odds are, it's going to be from the fungi
That lurk in the sinks of your local ER
Or some lobbyist's fancy foreign-made car.

Take heart and keep living! Get plenty of sleep!
Don't kayak in swamps! Don't ski where it's steep!
You can fret all you want to about the undead.
In the end you're likely to die in your bed.

In the end, you're likely to say to yourself,
As age leaves you sitting up on high on a shelf,
If I'd only done *more*, not stayed home and done less—
Seen Australia's reefs, and back-stroked Loch Ness!

It's a beautiful world, full of drama and dances,
A world full of choices but also of chances,
And nobody knows how they're gonna get through it.
There's no use in dread. Just get out and do it!

Coming Soon in Volume 2 of
Carson Clare's Trail Guide to Avoiding Death

Orthodontists/Maniacs (title still under consideration)
Algebra
Vampires
Puberty
Inadequate Cellular Networks

Made in the USA
Middletown, DE
30 August 2017